THIS IS FOR...

. . . .

WHO IS THE MOST
COLD ☐ FASCINATING ☐
OFFENSIVE ☐ CHEERY ☐
THRILLING ☐ MEAN ☐
DRAGON I KNOW
FROM

. . . .

PLEASE TICK WHERE APPROPRIATE

1

Grafton Books
A Division of the Collins Publishing Group
8 Grafton Street, London W1X 3LA

A Grafton Paperback Original 1987

ISBN 0-586-07487-2

Printed and bound in Great Britain by
Collins, Glasgow

Year of The Dragon

龍

Ian Heath

The Dragon...

...is sometimes a little clumsy

The Dragon...

...does not sleep well

The Dragon...

...can be heavy-handed

The Dragon...

...is terribly demanding

The Dragon...

...could be a supersalesman

The Dragon...

...is obsessed with perfection

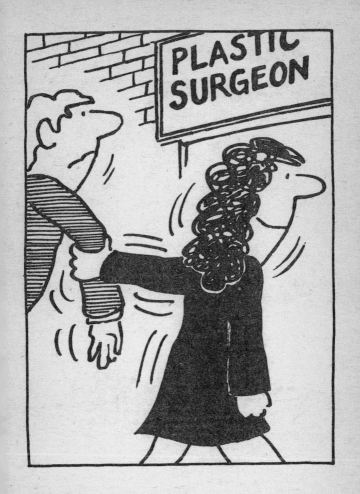

The Dragon...

...is very, very sociable

The
Dragon...

...can be
thoughtless

19

The
Dragon...

...can be rather
too open

The Dragon...

...is a high-achiever

23

The Dragon...

...hates television

The Dragon...

...hates competition

The Dragon...

...has difficulty remembering names

29

The Dragon...

...lacks a sense of humour

The
Dragon...

...loves uniforms

The Dragon...

...cannot stomach rice-pudding

35

The Dragon...

...has an impulsive streak

The Dragon...

...loves messing about in boats

39

The Dragon...

...could be a good hair stylist

The Dragon...

...has negative traits

The Dragon...

...is a keen fisherman

The Dragon...

...lacks vision

*The
Dragon...*

...takes pride in
his/her surroundings

49

The Dragon...

...has a steady hand

The Dragon...

...eats like a pig

The Dragon...

...is not blessed with patience

WOW!! THIS IS <u>THE</u> ONE!!

VERY SEXCITING!

THRILLS AND SPILLS!

AVERAGE TO LOUSY

TAKE TO THE HILLS-ALONE!

..DRAGON and RAT

NO PEACE,
BUT PLENTY OF PASSION
TO BE ENJOYED
BETWEEN THESE TWO.

...OX

TOO UNEMOTIONAL
TO LAST.

...TIGER

THE BEST PART FOR THIS
PAIR IS THE MAKING UP.

♡ ♡ ♡

...RABBIT

A QUICK, STEAMY FLING!

♡ ♡ ♡

..DRAGON

PLEASANT FOR A WHILE.

♡ ♡ ♡

...SNAKE

ALL THE INGREDIENTS
OF A SPICY AFFAIR
WITH A BRIGHT FUTURE.

...HORSE

GOOD FUN FOR A LONG
WEEKEND AWAY,
BUT PASSIONS WILL FADE
AS THE WEEK WEARS ON.
A PLEASANT INTERLUDE.

...SHEEP

UNHAPPILY ONE BIG YAWN

♡

..MONKEY

A PASSIONATE UNION!

♡ ♡ ♡ ♡ ♡

..ROOSTER

LOTS OF
HAPPILY-EVER-AFTERS

♡ ♡ ♡

...DOG

AN EXTREMELY
BRIEF ENCOUNTER,
BLINK,
AND YOU'LL MISS IT!

...PIG

PLENTY OF FROLICSOME
FUN FOR A COUPLE WHO
ARE ONLY TOO EAGER
TO PLEASE ONE ANOTHER.

Famous Dragons

FLORENCE NIGHTINGALE
HAILE SELASSIE · FATS WALLER
ANTHONY QUINN · ROALD DAHL
ZANDRA RHODES · BING CROSBY
SIGMUND FREUD · CHÉ GUEVARA
KIRK DOUGLAS · JEFFREY ARCHER
FAYE DUNAWAY · SHIRLEY TEMPLE
EDWARD HEATH · GREGORY PECK
GEORGE BERNARD SHAW
LEONARD WOOLF

SIR GORDON RICHARDS
JOHN LENNON · GLEN MILLER
BETTY GRABLE · CLIFF RICHARD
STANLEY KUBRICK · RINGO STARR
FRANK SINATRA · HAROLD WILSON
TOM JONES · YEHUDI MENUHIN
SARAH BERNHARDT · MAE WEST
GRAHAM GREENE · ST. JOAN OF ARC
VALERIE HARPER · SALVADOR DALI
WALTER MONDALE · PETER LORRE
JIMMY CONNORS · JOAN BAEZ
FRANCISCO FRANCO · GILES
QUEEN MARGARETHE II
KING CONSTANTINE